D1358979

COFFEE HIGH SCHOOL
159 TROJAN WAY
DOUGLAS, GA 31533

BRONCO BUSTER

Bronco buster /
F Bri   18793

Brin, Susannah.
        Coffee High School Media Center

SUSANNAH BRIN

TAKE TEN BOOKS

BY SUSANNAH BRIN

CHILLERS

THRILLERS

Development and Production: Laurel Associates, Inc.
Cover Illustrator: Black Eagle Productions

© 1998 Saddleback Publishing, Inc.

All rights reserved. No part of this publication may be reproduced or transmitted in any form without permission in writing from the publisher. Reproduction of any part of this book, through photocopy, recording, or any electronic or mechanical retrieval system, without the written permission of the publisher, is an infringement of copyright law.

SADDLEBACK
PUBLISHING • INC.

3505 Cadillac Ave., Building F-9
Costa Mesa, CA 92626

ISBN 1-56254-225-7

Printed in the United States of America
03 02 01 MM 01 00 CM 99 98   8 7 6 5 4 3 2 1

Contents

Chapter 1

Clay was eating a bowl of ice cream when he heard the slam of a truck door. He wasn't expecting anyone this early. Must be his older brother, Dylan, home early from the rodeo. Without bothering to put on a jacket against the morning cold, he ran outdoors to greet his brother.

When Clay rounded the side of the house, he saw Dylan standing in the driveway. A saddle was balanced on his shoulder, and a duffel bag was dangling from his hand. With that faraway look in his eyes, Clay thought Dylan looked like some kind of Western hero. But then he'd always thought Dylan was some kind of hero. It didn't bother him that his brother was taller and better looking than he was. He thought that was how it was supposed to be. "Hey, dude!" Clay called out. "I thought you'd never get back. Let me give you a hand with your gear."

Dylan didn't turn or say anything. He was staring past the house at the corral. A frown darkened his handsome face and made him look older than twenty. "Where'd those mustangs come from?" he asked.

Clay pushed his hands deep into his pockets and stared at the ground. Looking into Dylan's eyes when he was angry was like diving headfirst into a deep, icy pond. They made him shiver, those eyes.

"Me and Beback caught them up in Miner's Valley," Clay said softly.

"Well, get rid of them," Dylan said firmly as he walked past Clay and into the house.

Clay followed. "But I thought we

could break them and sell them. We need the money, Dylan. The bills are piling up. We're way behind on the mortgage payments, and . . ."

Dylan's eyes blazed blue-white with anger. "I *said* let them go! We don't have money to waste on feed, and I don't have time to break them. There's a rodeo somewhere almost every day now. What with driving and riding, I just don't have time."

"I know! That's why I thought *I* would break them. Beback said he'd help me," Clay said quickly.

"No, it's just too dangerous. And Beback's too old to be of any help. I don't know why he's putting you up to these schemes. I should have thrown him out when Ma and Pa were killed," grumbled Dylan. Yanking open the refrigerator door, he saw a couple of slices of old bologna and a carton of milk standing alone on the empty shelves of the refrigerator.

"Beback isn't putting me up to anything—really. Taming the mustangs was *my own* idea."

"No! If you get hurt, who'll be here to take care of you? And besides, this is your senior year, and I want you to graduate." Without another word, Dylan took the carton of milk from the refrigerator and drank from the carton.

"Don't drink that!" yelled Clay, but it was too late. Sour milk was already spraying out of his brother's mouth. Dylan swore, and Clay bit the inside of his mouth to keep from laughing. "I've been meaning to throw that out. I just didn't get to it."

"Just like you didn't get to these dishes," snapped Dylan, crossing to the sink. Dirty plates, greasy pans, and crumpled fast-food containers filled the sink and countertop.

"Believe me, I was going to clean up before you got back," Clay said, laughing nervously. "Remember the fuss Ma made when we dirtied her kitchen? Pa said the neighbors could hear her from miles away. And she'd never let us clean it up. She was afraid we'd make an even bigger mess."

"Yeah—but Ma's gone, Clay. She ain't ever coming back," sighed Dylan.

"I know, Dylan. I know that. And I was going to clean up in here, but . . ."

"But what? You've been too busy? I can't do it *all*, Clay. I'm busting my buns on the circuit trying to put food on the table and pay the mortgage. But I can't do it all."

"That's why I got the mustangs," Clay explained. "I know how hard you're trying. I want to help. We could surely use the money. Beback says it will be good experience for me to break the mustangs. That experience will count for a lot if I'm gonna join you on the rodeo circuit."

"Join me on the circuit? Where did you get an idea like that?"

"The rodeo is in *my* blood, too! Granddad was a bronc rider. And so was Pa—at least he was until he started breeding stock for the rodeos. I thought I could come on the circuit with you. You know, get my feet wet. It'd be just like old times," said Clay.

"Forget it," Dylan snapped. "We're never going to ride the circuit together. The rodeo has already claimed two Davidsons, and that's enough." His voice was low and sad. Clay took a step toward his brother.

"It was an *accident* that killed them, Dylan. Not the rodeo."

Dylan didn't say anything for several seconds. A gulf of silence separated the two brothers, and Clay didn't know how to cross it. Finally, Dylan turned and looked out the window. "Just do as I say. Get rid of the mustangs, Clay."

"But I want to help . . ."

"No. I don't need your help. You

just concentrate on graduating." He pulled a twenty from his pocket and dropped it on the table. "If you want to help, you can buy some groceries and clean up this pigsty. I'm going to Spokane for a week. They got a small county rodeo starting up there. I think I've got a good chance of winning. And one more thing—I *mean* it about those horses. They've got to go, Clay."

Clay watched his older brother walk away. He heard the front door slam, and then the pickup turning in the driveway. His chest felt heavy, crowded with anger and sadness and all the things he had wanted to say.

Out back, he heard a mustang whinny. Turning, he looked out the kitchen window. The mustang nodded its head in his direction and shook its mane. Clay grabbed his jacket from its hook and headed out to the corral.

Chapter 2

Rope in hand, Clay climbed over the fence and dropped down into the soft dirt. The three mustangs galloped away and bunched together at the other end of the corral. Clay uncoiled his rope as he walked toward the frightened wild horses. His plan was to lasso one of the horses, then drive the other two into the smaller corral.

Clay tried to decide which would be the easiest to tackle first. Two of the horses, a red and a gray, were about the same height. The third horse, a black mare with a splash of white on its forehead, towered above the other two. For protection, the smaller horses huddled together behind the black mare. As Clay approached, the big horse stood its ground. Its body was quivering, ears thrown back, eyes rolling. The black mustang was clearly a horse to be feared. Clay decided to get the small red first.

Clay flicked his wrist and sent his lasso flying through the air. The rope settled around the neck of the small red mustang. Quickly, Clay yanked on the rope and pulled the lasso tight. Digging his heels into the dirt, he held on as the red mustang reared back, squealing with fear. It pulled against the rope, twisting first one way, then the other. The rope cut into Clay's hands, but he didn't care. There was no way he was going to let go of it.

Suddenly, the little red mustang charged. It reared back and brought its front legs crashing down—inches from Clay's body. Caught off guard, Clay staggered back and fell. His head hit the ground with a numbing thud. While he still kept hold of the rope, the red horse began to rear up again.

Horrified, Clay saw the horse's hooves dancing in the air above him. Everything seemed to be happening in slow motion. Then a warning voice in his brain cried out. Finally, letting go of the rope, he rolled out of the way. In the next second, the horse pounded its front legs down on the spot where Clay's head had just been. Then the little red whinnied loudly as it raced off to join the other horses.

Clay stood up and dusted himself off. His legs felt weak and his head ached. Breaking the horses wasn't going to be as easy as he'd thought. For the first time, fear played with Clay's mind and made him question what he was doing. Maybe Dylan *did* know best. Maybe he should just let the mustangs go free. What if he got badly hurt? Wouldn't that just make it harder on all of them? Lost in his own thoughts, Clay was suddenly startled to see

Beback standing by the gate.

"You been wrestling with those horses, or what?" asked Beback. A hint of a smile played across his face.

Clay looked down at his dusty clothes, then back at the old cowboy. "Yeah, something like that," he mumbled, wondering just how much Beback had seen. He didn't want Beback to see his fear, his indecision. The old cowboy had worked on and off for his family for as long as he could remember. When his parents had been killed in the truck accident, Beback had stayed on to help out.

"I see you lassoed the red," said Beback, making conversation.

"Yeah." Clay really didn't feel all that much like talking.

"I guess all those months you spent roping fence posts paid off."

"Uh huh."

Neither of them spoke. The horses nickered and pawed the ground. Clay glanced sideways at Beback. The old man's face was wrinkled from years of working outdoors in all kinds of weather. But it was still a good-looking face—tough and honest. Right now he was chewing on a piece of straw, something he did when he was doing what he called "serious thinking." Clay guessed that Beback's "serious thinking" had something to do with him and the wild horses.

Clay squirmed uncomfortably. Then he took a deep breath and said, "I was trying to separate the mustangs." When Beback didn't say anything, Clay continued. "That red mare isn't nearly as gentle as she looks."

"No wild thing is gentle until it's been tamed, boy," said Beback. He slowly moved the straw from one corner of his mouth to the other.

Clay stared at the red mare. The lasso around its neck was still secure. He knew he should take the lasso off the horse before it hurt itself. But his fear kept him on the fence.

If Beback noticed the tangled rope, he didn't say anything about it. He seemed content to just sit on the fence and watch the clouds drift by.

Clay cleared his throat. "Dylan told me to get rid of the horses. He doesn't want me trying to break them. He's afraid I'll get hurt or something."

"Is that what's stopping you from finishing what you started this fine morning?" asked Beback. The old man's eyes danced with amusement.

"No. I just got to thinking that maybe Dylan's right after all," said Clay defensively.

A few years back Dylan had broken his leg in two places. He'd been thrown from a bucking horse in this same corral. Clay remembered how he'd lain on the ground, crying and wiggling like a squashed bug. His parents had been alive then. For several months, Ma had taken care of Dylan. If Clay broke his leg, who'd take care of him? And with their dad gone, who would make him get back on a horse when his body had finally mended?

"Sure would be a shame to turn them horses loose," Beback muttered. "Especially after all the trouble we went to getting them."

"Well, maybe it wasn't such a good idea in the first place," snapped Clay. Turning away, he jumped down from the fence and started for the house.

"You can't run from your fear, Clay-boy. The only way to beat it is to just face it head on," said Beback, shaking his head.

Clay didn't want to hear Beback's advice. The only sound he wanted to hear was the banging of the screen door behind him as he went home.

Chapter 3

It was late in the afternoon when Clay walked back out to the corral. He had tried to forget about the mustangs, but everything in the house, from the pictures on the walls to the trophies gathering dust on the shelves, reminded him of who he was. He was the son of a rodeo rider. The son of a man who, after leaving the circuit, had devoted his life to breeding rodeo stock.

Clay knew that if his father hadn't died, he would have taught him how to break horses, how to ride a bronc. His father had taught Dylan. But Dylan, he knew, would never teach him.

When he got to the main corral, Clay was surprised to see the red mare all alone. The other horses were in the back corral. He shook his head and laughed. "That old coot!" he said aloud.

He found Beback sitting in the tack room, working on a piece of rope.

"What are you doing?" asked Clay.

Beback didn't look up. "Tying knots in this here rope. The way I figure it, we got a week to break those horses and sell them before your brother gets back. A week isn't much time to gentle a horse and get it used to a saddle. So we'll have to break them the old way."

"How'd you know that I'd change my mind?"

"You've never been a quitter, Clay. I reckoned you just needed a little time to see your way through your fear," answered Beback.

"I'm still afraid," admitted Clay.

"Good. Only a fool wouldn't be afraid of a thousand pounds of moving, kicking, rearing bone and muscle. A horse can be a dangerous animal when it's frightened."

"I know," said Clay.

"Besides, a little fear can help you. Give you that edge," added Beback. He stood up and twirled the rope he had been working on. It looked just like the lasso that Clay had used earlier, only smaller in width. Beback worked the slipknot back and forth several times, checking it for speed and smoothness.

"What are we going to use that little lasso for?" asked Clay.

"Come on, I'll show you." Beback picked up a halter and a set of reins. He motioned to Clay to grab the saddle.

"I think we should wait until tomorrow. The sun will be going down in another hour or so," said Clay. He threw the saddle over the rail and looked at Beback. The old man was already climbing into the corral.

Beback flashed Clay a devilish grin. "I think you should try *doing* instead of *thinking* for a while. Now just sit there until I call for you." Beback turned and walked towards the red mare.

The red mare was pushing hard against the fence. She wanted to join the other horses in the back pen. Clay frowned. He wondered if it'd been such a good idea to separate them. One of the basic needs of a horse was to be with other horses. By separating the red mare from the others, he may have made the mare even wilder and harder to handle.

Clay watched as Beback approached the red horse from its blind side. Slowly, the old man moved closer and closer until he was only a few feet from the frightened animal. Clay was worried. He knew that Beback couldn't get out of the way if the horse turned on him. He held his breath as Beback sent his lasso spinning toward the horse's front feet.

The lasso seemed to skim too close to the ground. But as the mare started to run, the rope slithered up her front legs! Surprised, the horse stumbled and started to fall. Beback quickly jerked on the rope, forcing the horse to go down. *So* that's *how you "jerk down" a horse,* thought Clay. Then Beback ran over and quickly hogtied the horse's legs.

"Bring the saddle, boy," yelled Beback as he stood up.

Clay slid off the fence and hit the ground running. He stopped not too far from Beback and looked down at the frightened, struggling horse.

"Now what we're going to do is put this here saddle on the mare while she's down. Then I'm going to untie her feet. And as she gets up, you're going to jump up onto her back," instructed Beback.

Clay stared at Beback in disbelief.

"Don't just stand there with your mouth open, boy! Help me get this saddle on," Beback ordered, snatching the saddle blanket from Clay's hands.

The sharpness of Beback's tone forced Clay to forget his fear. Instead, he concentrated on getting the saddle on the thrashing horse. All the while, the horse squealed with fear and squirmed on the ground like a snake.

After the mare was saddled, Beback motioned for Clay to come stand by him. "Now as I untie these ropes, she's going to start to get up. That's when you mount her." Beback started to untie the ropes.

"Now!" yelled Beback, quickly releasing the ropes.

Clay had barely seated himself in the saddle when the red mare started to buck and kick. She leapt into the air and bowed her body like a diver doing a jackknife off a diving board.

When the mare uncoiled and leapt into the air, Clay lost his grip. A second later, he flew through the air and hit the ground hard with a thud. He sat watching as the red mare galloped off to the far end of the corral. Before he could stand up, Beback was at his side.

"You okay?" Beback asked. Clay was touched by the concern in the old cowboy's voice.

"Yeah," said Clay, dusting himself off and trying to smile.

"Good. I'll get the mare. You got to get right back on, you know."

"What?" yelped Clay. The last thing he wanted to do was get back on that crazy horse. But he did. He got back on again and again. The third time he was bucked off, Clay landed face down in the dirt. Slowly, carefully, he rolled over onto his back. His body felt like he'd been run over by a truck. Blood trickled from the corner of his mouth.

"I think you've had enough for today," said Beback matter-of-factly. "Besides, it's getting dark." He put out his hand and pulled Clay to his feet.

Clay groaned as he straightened up.

"You done good for your first time,

Clay. I wish we had more light. That mare needs to be ridden until she stops bucking. Otherwise, she might get to thinking she's pretty smart for throwing you," said Beback with a grin.

"Uh huh," said Clay as he gingerly took a step forward.

"No matter, boy. We'll try again tomorrow. You go on in to the house now, and I'll unsaddle her," said Beback, giving Clay a playful slap on the back.

Clay let out a yelp of pain. Then, hunched over like a little old man, he walked toward the house.

"Soak in a hot bath. You'll be fine by morning!" Beback yelled out.

Right. I'll be lucky if I live that long, thought Clay as he carefully lowered his aching body over the fence.

Chapter 4

Clay knew what he had to do. The next day, he got back on the red mare. At first it bucked and kicked and raged. Finally, played out, the mare got used to having a rider on her back.

Clay tackled the gray horse next. Again, the same things happened. The gray bucked and hurled itself into the air, fighting to shake off the burden on its back. Again and again, Clay was thrown from the saddle. At the end of the day, he figured he'd spent more time on the ground than he had on the horse. But he persisted.

The following days passed in a blur of work and pain. Clay's body seemed permanently bruised and sore. Most mornings, it was all he could do to drag himself out of bed to go to school. But by the time he got home in the afternoon, he was actually looking forward to climbing on the back of a wild horse. Clay hadn't stopped being afraid, but the excitement and the danger drew him like a magnet. And for the first time in his life, he felt good about himself. Beback taught him how to stay on longer by gripping the horse tightly with his knees.

A harder lesson was learning to keep his hands away from the saddle. Sometimes, when he was starting to fall, he wanted to grab hold of the saddlehorn. But he knew that if he wanted to compete in the rodeo, he couldn't do that. Rodeo rules were very clear. A rider would be immediately disqualified for pulling leather—in other words, grabbing the saddlehorn. So Clay learned to resist the impulse.

One afternoon Clay was cantering

around the corral on the gray mare when he saw a truck and horse trailer pull up. He looked over at Beback, who was sitting on the fence.

"What's Travelson doing here, Beback?"

"Oh, I was talking to him in town today. He said he needed two more mares. I told him we had two green-broke horses for sale," explained Beback.

"I didn't think they were ready," said Clay. He had wanted to go on working them for a few more days.

"They're as ready as we've got time for. You're forgetting your brother is gonna be back soon. You still have to break the black."

Clay turned in the saddle and glanced at the black horse. It was galloping wildly back and forth the length of the corral. A week in captivity hadn't calmed it a bit. It was as wild and highstrung as the day they'd trapped it. But now, Clay knew, he couldn't wait any longer to break the black. This horse wouldn't be as easy to tame as the other two. It was clear that the big black mare was a real fighter. Both fear and excitement mingled together in the pit of Clay's stomach.

"Well, boy, are we going to sell these horses or not?" asked Beback impatiently. If he knew why Clay seemed hesitant, he didn't let on.

"Yes, sir. But you make the deal. I want to see a real horse trader in action," teased Clay. He flashed Beback a big grin and trotted off toward the gate. Looking back over his shoulder, Clay could see Beback talking with Mr. Travelson. Beback was pointing and gesturing toward Clay and the horse.

"Bring her on up here," hollered Beback.

Clay nudged the gray lightly in the sides with his boots. The horse kicked out with its hind legs, so Clay quickly spun the horse first in one direction and then the other to distract it. When the horse finally settled down, he rode toward Beback and Travelson.

"Come on, Sam. You know as well as I do that no range horse is worth having if it doesn't buck once in a while," said Beback.

"That's what all you oldtimers say. But times have changed. People these days want gentle, well-behaved horses," said Sam Travelson. He frowned as he eyed the gray.

"With a little more work, this horse will be as gentle as a kitten. I told you right up front that these horses are only green-broke," said Beback.

"Look, I'll give you four hundred for the both of them," said Travelson.

"Come *on!* We could get that much at the dog food factory," lied Beback. "Now if you're talking four hundred *each*, then maybe we can do business."

"Three twenty-five," countered

Travelson, with a sly glint in his eye.

"Now I know you didn't bring that trailer all the way over here for nothing. Three seventy-five," said Beback. He glanced sideways at Clay and winked. Clay grinned.

"You drive a hard bargain, Beback. But you got yourself a deal," said Travelson, stepping away from the fence. He reached into his pocket and pulled out a wad of bills. Then he slowly counted out seven hundred and fifty dollars and handed the pile of bills to Beback.

Clay helped the two men load the mares into the trailer. After Travelson locked the trailer doors, he shook hands with Beback and Clay. "Nice doing business with you," he said as he climbed into the cab of his truck. He slammed the cab door and looked out at Clay. "Beback tells me you're a natural bronco buster, son. Your daddy would be real proud."

"Why, thank you, sir," said Clay. He could feel himself grinning crazily, but he couldn't help it. Just knowing that Beback thought he was a natural bronco buster made his heart swell with pride and happiness. As Travelson drove down the road, Beback turned to Clay and handed him the money from the sale of the horses.

Clay looked at the money, then at his old friend. "You know I can't take all of this, Beback. Why, we're *partners*, remember?" said Clay.

"Take it. Consider it rent money or something," mumbled Beback.

"But it's not *right*. You got to take half," argued Clay. Beback leaned against the corral and stared at the black horse.

"Come on, Beback, take your share," insisted Clay.

"Look, if you all lose this ranch, I'll have to look for a new place to hang my hat. So just consider my share as my way of helping out," said Beback, roughly.

Clay hesitated. He sure didn't like keeping Beback's share. But he knew there was no use arguing with the old man once he made up his mind. He shoved the money into his pocket. "Thanks. I won't forget this," said Clay.

Beback didn't answer. Studying the sky, he was watching big black clouds gather over the distant mountains. A storm was coming. "When did you say Dylan was getting back?" asked Beback.

"I don't expect him for a couple more days," answered Clay. "I sure hope it doesn't rain tomorrow."

Beback laughed. "Why? You afraid of getting throwed in the mud?"

"No. I'm afraid of that big horse slipping in the mud and falling on me."

Chapter 5

The next morning, the sky was gray and cloudy when Clay left the house and headed down to the corral. He shivered and buttoned his jacket against the morning chill. Sometime during the night, it had rained. Water dripped from the edge of the roof and pooled in puddles in the driveway.

Clay frowned. He didn't have to see the corral to know that the rain had turned it into a sloshy mud pie. He cursed his luck. There was no time to let it dry out before he broke the black horse. Dylan would be home any day.

The black horse stood in the middle of the corral with its rump toward the wind. Its black coat was damp and shiny. When it saw Clay, it raised its head and threw back its ears. Alert to danger, the black was tense and jumpy.

"I see the rain didn't dampen your spirits," muttered Clay. This horse, he knew, would fight him tooth and nail. Just thinking about walking over to the horse made his heart beat faster.

"You're up early. Can't wait to get on that horse, huh?" said Beback with a grin. His arms were loaded with a bunch of gear.

Clay laughed, reaching out to help his old friend. He took the saddle and placed it on the fence rail.

"Put these on," said Beback. He held up a pair of leather chaps.

"I don't need those. I reckon my jeans will wash."

Beback threw Clay a questioning look, and then he roared with laughter. "These aren't to keep the mud off ya. They're to help you stay on the horse, boy. Give you a better grip."

"Oh, right. I knew that," said Clay, pretending that he'd known all along why Beback wanted him to wear the seatless leather trousers.

"And they'll protect your legs, too," added Beback as he jumped down into the corral.

Clay pulled the chaps over his jeans. He wished he'd had them earlier in the week. The skin on the inside of his legs was still bruised and raw.

Beback didn't have an easy time roping the black horse. It was fast and smart, dodging first right, then left. Finally, Beback got off a good swing of the rope. Then he yanked hard, tightening the lasso around the black's front legs. As he jerked it down into the mud, the black horse squealed and screamed like a raging bull. Mud splattered Clay's face as he helped saddle the downed horse. He could feel the black puffing out its stomach as Beback pulled the girth tighter. *Smart horse,* Clay thought. He glanced at Beback to see if the old man had noticed the horse expanding its stomach. He didn't want to get into the saddle and have it slip loose when the horse exhaled. But Clay didn't have to worry. Beback was already working the cinch up another notch.

Clay swung up into the saddle just as the black horse struggled to get to its feet. Whipping its head around, the horse glared at Clay and then leapt high in the air. When it landed back on the ground, the angry horse twisted its body and jumped again.

Clay held the reins in one hand and waved his other hand in the air—for balance, as Beback had taught him. But balance wasn't enough with a horse like the black. Soon Clay found himself flying through the air.

This time, Clay didn't need Beback to tell him to get back on. He wiped the mud from his face and ran across the corral to where Beback had the fighting horse cornered. But just as he stepped into the stirrup, the horse took off running.

Clay held on to the saddlehorn with both hands, his body pressed against the horse's side. He tried to mount but couldn't. When the black reached the fence it turned quickly, wedging Clay between the fence and its own body. Clay let go of the saddlehorn and reached for the fence. As he leaned out, the black spun around, raised its hind legs, and kicked him. Clay fell over the fence and landed in the mud outside the corral.

That big horse means to kill me, thought Clay, spitting out pebbles and dirt. He sat up. He started to wipe his face with the back of his arm but then realized that it wouldn't do any good. Every inch of his body was covered with mud.

"Are you hurt?" Beback asked.

Hunkering down next to Clay, he studied the young man's face.

"No—just my pride," answered Clay. "I didn't even get a chance to swing up into the saddle."

Beback took off the red bandanna he wore around his neck and handed it to Clay. "No matter how good you get, there's always going to be some horse that's better."

Clay stood up. A big raindrop fell on his face and rolled down his neck. He looked up at the sky and saw that it was crowded with dark puffy clouds that looked ready to burst open. The black horse whinnied. "What's so darn funny?" Clay yelled at the horse. He climbed back into the corral.

All of a sudden, a bolt of lightning zigzagged across the sky. "Clay, I think we should call it a day," hollered Beback.

The sound of thunder crashing through the sky frightened the black. It reared and danced on its hind legs. As it brought its front legs down on the ground, Clay grabbed the halter. He pulled the horse's head to the side until its nose almost touched his leg. Then he swung up into the saddle. The horse kicked. Then it bucked slightly and started spinning around and around in tight circles. Clay gripped harder with his legs.

When the horse couldn't buck Clay off, it tried to run out from under him. This time Clay was ready. He reined sharply to the right. The horse jerked and kicked. But then the black slipped. As the big horse fell slowly toward the ground, Clay tried to throw himself from the saddle. But he was too late. Suddenly, he was under the horse. Air exploded from his chest as hundreds of pounds of horseflesh rolled across his body. The last thing he heard was a popping sound and someone yelling. Then everything went black.

Chapter 6

Clay opened his eyes to find Beback's face just inches from his own. He smiled weakly, trying to dispel the worry he saw on his friend's face. "Guess I must have passed out," Clay said, sitting up.

"Anything feel broken?" asked Beback, worriedly.

"I don't think so."

Beback turned toward the corral gate and yelled, "He's fine. Just got the wind knocked out of him."

Clay looked toward the corral and saw Dylan leaning on the gate. Even though Dylan was several yards away, Clay could see the scowl on his brother's face. *Shoot, he's back early*, thought Clay as he scrambled to his feet. When he wobbled, Beback reached out his hand to steady him. Clay shrugged off Beback's help. "When did Dylan get here?" he asked in a low voice as they headed for the gate.

"Oh, I guess it was just about the time the black decided to roll over on you," answered Beback.

"Great. Just great," muttered Clay. He knew he was in for it now.

As Clay and Beback approached the gate, Dylan stepped away from the gate post. Clay saw why his brother was home early. Dylan's left leg was in a plaster cast from the knee down.

"I thought I could trust you to do what I told you," barked Dylan. His mouth was set in a hard thin line, and his eyes burned with anger.

"We broke the red and the gray. Got seven-fifty for them," explained Clay. "A few more days and the black would be broke to the saddle and . . ."

"And out of here before I got home,

right?" Dylan said harshly.

The fierceness of his brother's stare made Clay look away. "Not exactly. I just thought the money we got for the horses would make up for not doing like you said," mumbled Clay. He shuffled his feet and silently chided himself for being so afraid of Dylan's anger and disapproval.

"Come on, Dylan!" Beback said. "No harm's been done. Clay was bound to learn how to break horses one of these days."

"No *harm's* been done? Is that what you said?" Dylan gestured wildly with his crutch.

"Yup. Clay's worked real hard this week. And I think he's done good," said Beback calmly. He shot Clay a look of encouragement.

"Oh yeah?" Dylan snorted. "That black horse could have killed him a few minutes ago. So why don't you just mind your business, old man?" Without another word, Dylan positioned the crutches under his arms and hobbled off toward the house.

Clay threw Beback a worried look.

"He'll simmer down once he's thought it through," said Beback.

"I don't know. He's pretty angry," said Clay, staring after his brother.

A few drops of rain fell, and then, without further warning, the whole sky opened up. "You want to come up to the house, Beback?" asked Clay.

"Go on," Beback replied. "This is between you and your brother. I'll catch up with you all later."

Through sheets of rain, Clay made a headlong dash for the back door. Ducking quickly into the kitchen, he shrugged off his wet clothes and boots. Muddy water streamed onto the clean floor. From the banging sounds at the back of the house, he figured Dylan was in his room. Clay glanced around the kitchen. He saw that the trash can was empty, everything was clean, and the refrigerator was filled with food. *Nothing for Dylan to complain about*, Clay thought as he headed for the shower.

Later, as Clay stood at the stove frying two hamburgers, Dylan thumped into the kitchen. He fell in a chair and dropped his crutches on the floor. The sound of hamburgers frying mingled with the splash of the rain against the windows. Finally, Clay broke the silence. "You want a hamburger?"

"Okay," said Dylan, without looking up. A peace offering, the money from the sale of the mares, lay on the table.

Clay laid out the food, pulled back a chair, and sat down opposite his brother. Then he busied himself with slopping catsup and mayonnaise on his hamburger bun.

"I'm sorry I got so upset earlier," Dylan mumbled between bites.

"Forget it," Clay said nonchalantly. Inwardly, he sighed with relief. Maybe

Dylan was finally coming around to seeing things his way.

"When I saw that horse sit down on top of you, well . . . I just don't want you getting yourself hurt, Clay. You got school and . . ."

"How'd you break your leg?" asked Clay, changing the subject.

"My fault. I sat too far back in the saddle. Back near the brace. Anyway, I spurred the horse and hollered for them to open the chute door. But before they could open it, that darn horse bucked. It bucked me right into the arena— about twenty feet from the chute. When I landed, my leg twisted under me."

"You mean the horse reared up on the slope? In the chute?" asked Clay.

"Kicked out its hindquarters and really sent me flying!" Dylan laughed. "Bad luck that I landed on my weak leg. And now I'll have to miss the rodeo tomorrow over in Vern County. Losing my entry fee hurts just about as much as this leg does."

"Don't worry. We've got the money from the sale of the two mares," said Clay. Then he paused, picking his words carefully. "And the black should bring a good price once I break her." He was just about to add that he could take Dylan's place at the Vern County Rodeo. But the look on his brother's face stopped him.

"No. You are *not* getting back on that black horse! I'm home now and what I say goes," thundered Dylan. He angrily slapped the table so hard the dishes rattled.

Clay shoved his chair back and stood up. "Oh, yeah? I *am* going to tame that horse. And you're not going to stop me!" He glared at his brother.

"We'll see about that," said Dylan, his voice cold as ice.

"Yeah, we will." Clay held Dylan's gaze for a moment then stomped off.

Chapter 7

When Clay awoke the next morning, the rain had stopped and the sky was clear and blue. As he dressed, he thought about his fight with Dylan the night before. Their argument didn't sit well with him. Oh, sure, they'd had plenty of arguments before. But this one was different somehow. Pulling a thick sweater over his shirt, he headed for the kitchen.

Clay was surprised to see Dylan already sitting at the table, reading the sports page. "You're up early," Clay said, grabbing the orange juice bottle.

"Couldn't sleep. Couldn't find a comfortable position," Dylan answered.

"Yeah, I bet that cast is really awkward," said Clay. He leaned against the counter and tried to gauge Dylan's mood. "Looks like it's going to be a real nice day."

"Cold."

Now how did he know that, Clay wondered, *unless he's already been outside.* The thought that Dylan might have released the black horse sent a flash of anger through Clay's body.

No, Dylan wouldn't do that, he reasoned. The newpaper rustled as Dylan turned the page. Clay sighed. The paper. That was it. Dylan had gone out to get the paper off the porch. Pulling on his cowboy boots, Clay saw that they were caked with dried mud from the day before. "I think I'll mosey on down to the barn."

"Wear a jacket," Dylan answered, without looking up.

Ignoring his brother's advice, Clay went outside. The cold stung his face and made his eyes water. Rounding the corner of the house, he stopped suddenly. *The corral was empty.*

Clay ran toward the barn. *Maybe Beback moved the black mare into a stall,* he thought, not wanting to believe the worst.

Clay raced through the empty barn. His heart beating wildly, he ran to the bunkhouse and banged loudly on the door.

Beback peeked out and muttered, "What the—"

"The black horse is *gone!* Did you move it?" panted Clay.

"No," said Beback. Clay saw the look of surprise on the old man's face. He knew Beback was telling the truth. That meant that Dylan had freed the mustang. With an angry grunt, he turned back to the house.

Dylan, leaning on his crutches, was standing at the kitchen sink when Clay stormed in.

"You had no right to free the black," said Clay angrily.

"I'm just trying to look out for you, little brother," answered Dylan calmly.

"I don't need you or anyone else to take care of me," hissed Clay, running from the kitchen.

"Come back here!" yelled Dylan as he hobbled after Clay, who had disappeared into his bedroom.

Clay grabbed a duffle bag and quickly threw some clothes into it. "Where do you think you're going?" asked Dylan, blocking the doorway.

Clay zipped up his bag and started toward the door. "As far away from you as possible. Now get out of my way," he said, looking his brother straight in the eye.

Suddenly Dylan's hand snaked out and grabbed him by the front of his sweater. Without thinking, Clay reacted. His free hand swung around, catching Dylan under the chin. Dylan stumbled back against the hall wall. Then, as Clay advanced, his brother lashed out with his crutch, catching Clay sharply in the side.

Like a wildcat, Clay leaped forward and knocked his brother down. Dylan's crutches clattered noisily as they fell on the hardwood floor. Distracted by the noise, Dylan loosened his grip. Clay pushed him away and stood up. Grabbing the crutches and his bag, he headed for the front door.

"Where do you think you're going?" yelled Dylan, struggling to get up.

"To find me a bronc to bust," Clay snapped angrily. He yanked open the front door and tossed the crutches into the yard. As he walked toward Dylan's pickup, he didn't look back.

Chapter 8

Clay's anger took him all the way to the registration booth at the Vern County Rodeo. But it was his proud determination and fast talking that took over from there. Convincing the rodeo officials to replace his brother's name with his on the entry card wasn't easy. But it saved him the fee in the bronco-busting event. Now he glanced down at the card. "Number twenty. All right," he said happily as he walked toward the back of the arena.

Clay flashed his number at the man guarding the gate that led to the pens and chutes. When the guard motioned for him to enter, Clay felt a rush of pride. He straightened his shoulders, nodded at the guard, and entered the backstage world of the rodeo cowboy. It wasn't the first time. He had been in the staging area with his father hundreds of times, in many different places. But this was something else. He was a *competitor* now.

As he walked past the groups of cowboys, Clay grinned and tipped his hat. It was no surprise that he didn't recognize any of the contestants. Vern County Rodeo was too small to attract many riders from the professional circuit, unless they just happened to be in the area. Clay was glad it was small. That meant there were no qualifying rounds to get through.

Sitting down on a bench near the wall, he opened his bag. He pulled out a pair of dull-pointed spurs and looked at them for a moment. They had belonged to his father.

"I sure hope you don't mind my borrowing them, Pa," he said softly. He had always imagined that when his day came to compete, his parents and his brother would be rooting for him in the stands. He shook his head and blinked back the tears that sprang to his eyes whenever he thought of his parents.

Suddenly, the voice of the rodeo announcer boomed throughout the stadium. The rodeo was starting. A cowboy on a white horse galloped into the arena. He carried the American flag. Clay stood at attention as the announcer led the crowd in singing "The Star Spangled Banner" and "The Cowboy Prayer." Then came the rodeo parade of stock contractors, pickup men, and the pretty young rodeo queen and her court.

As the parade wound through the arena, Clay bent down and attached the spurs to his boots. His fingers shook as he fastened the buckles. Then he stood up and stomped first one foot, then the other. The spurs made a tinkling sound like jinglebells. Clay checked and rechecked his spurs. They spun easily and the points were dull. A rider could be disqualified for wearing spurs that were locked into position or were too sharp. Satisfied that his spurs were fine, he scrambled up onto a riser to get a better view.

"Ladies and gentlemen, we are going to start off our rodeo with one of the rough stock events—saddle bronco riding. And as I read off the names of the contestants, I will also read off the name of the horse they've drawn. So listen up, all you buckaroos back in the chute area," boomed the voice of the announcer.

Clay crossed his fingers and prayed for the luck of the draw. It was very important to get a good bronco. He knew that the judges rated the rider not only on how long he could stay on, but on the difficulty of the horse. Some cowboys believed that the luck of the draw was as important as ability. Finally, Clay heard his name. He had drawn a horse called Outlaw.

A cowboy sitting nearby hollered at him. "You got a good draw, kid. Outlaw is one wild bucking machine."

"That's great," said Clay, grinning nervously.

He watched as the first contestant signaled for the chute to be opened. When it did, the cowboy and bucking horse raced into the arena. In only a moment the rearing horse started bucking, sending its rider sailing through the air. Two pickup men rode into the ring and helped the downed cowboy to his feet. "That was Bill Weathers from Vern County. He was riding Jester. Bill's time was two seconds. Let's give him a big hand for coming down here and trying," the announcer urged the crowd.

Clay cringed. To be in the running,

a rider needed to stay on at least eight seconds. As the second rider gave the signal to release the chute, Clay jumped down from the fence. He was too nervous and jumpy to watch. He paced back and forth the length of the hallway. Mentally, he reviewed all the things Beback had taught him. He shook his arms and hands, trying to release the tension building in his body.

Then a commotion at the contestant gate broke Clay's concentration. When he turned to see what was happening, he was surprised to see Dylan and Beback. Dylan was arguing with the guard, who refused to let him enter. Not wanting his brother to see him, Clay turned and headed for the animal pens. But it was too late—Dylan had already spotted him.

"Clay!" shouted Dylan, waving at him to come over.

Slowly, Clay turned to face his

brother. "You can't stop me, Dylan!" he yelled before turning and heading over toward the chutes.

"Clay, will you listen to me? I . . ."

The crowd roared, drowning out Dylan's words. Clay bit the side of his lip. He would show his brother that he had what it took to be a bronco buster. *Maybe then*, he thought, *he'll realize I'm not a kid anymore.*

Then the announcer called Clay's number. His heart skipped a beat. He ran to the chute and climbed down into the tiny stall. As he lowered his body into the saddle, he could feel the buckskin-colored horse tremble with energy. He positioned his legs with his spurs above the horse's shoulders. According to the rules, the rider's spurs had to touch the horse's shoulders as it left the chute. Beback had called it "marking him out."

Clay gripped the reins with his left hand. "Okay, Outlaw. Show me what you've got," Clay cried as he signaled for the chute man to open the gate.

The horse exploded from the chute like a comet streaking through the sky. It leapt into the air and hunched up its back, jumping and twisting its body. Clay waved his right arm in the air and gripped hard with his legs. He felt like he was riding a tornado.

Several brief, brutal seconds ticked by as Clay struggled to stay on the bucking horse. Somewhere in the distance, he could hear the crowd yelling, "Ride 'em cowboy!" The big horse continued to jump and whip its head like a dog shaking water from its fur. Then, all of a sudden, the horse shuddered all over and landed hard. A buzzer sounded.

"Yahoo!" yelled Clay, realizing he'd gone the required eight seconds. Then the wild bronco jumped again and Clay threw himself off, landing hard on the arena floor. The horse was already on its feet. When it started to kick its hind legs toward Clay, a pickup man quickly rode between Clay and the kicking buckskin.

Clay stood up. He wanted to scream and holler and jump up and down in joy. *He had done it.*

"Ten seconds for Clay Davidson," the announcer called out. "That puts him in the lead. Good ride, cowboy!"

Clay waved at the crowd as he stepped out of the arena. Cowboys slapped him on the back and praised his ride. He grinned and took it all in. Nothing could have made him happier than he was at that moment. Then he heard the sound of his brother's voice calling his name.

"Clay."

He turned and saw Dylan bearing down on him as fast his crutches would allow him to go. Beback was right beside him.

"You *did* it, boy!" cried Beback,

pushing past Dylan and slapping Clay on the back. "Good riding!"

"Good teacher," said Clay. Then he glanced nervously at his brother. Dylan flashed him a big smile.

"What do you think?" asked Clay. He looked down at his boots.

"I think I'm looking at a future world champion bronco buster," Dylan said softly.

Clay looked up at him in surprise. "I thought . . . I thought you didn't want me to compete."

"Well, I guess a man's got to do what a man's got to do." Dylan winked at Beback. "*After* graduation, that is," he added quickly.

"Whatever you say, Dylan. You're the big brother," said Clay.

"And don't you forget it," Dylan laughed, giving him a playful jab with the end of his crutch. Then, in a serious voice, he went on, "And I won't forget that you're not a kid anymore."

Clay smiled at his brother. He couldn't remember when he'd felt so happy. Glancing back at the arena—where a cowboy was struggling to ride a wild bull—he knew that he would never forget this day for as long as he lived.